SCHOLASTIC

10 MINUTE SATs TESTS

3 subjects in 1

GRAMMAR, READING AND MATHS

YEAR 3

AGES 7–8

Scholastic Education, an imprint of Scholastic Ltd
Book End, Range Road, Witney, Oxfordshire, OX29 0YD
Registered office: Westfield Road, Southam, Warwickshire CV47 0RA
www.scholastic.co.uk

© 2019, Scholastic Ltd

1 2 3 4 5 6 7 8 9   9 0 1 2 3 4 5 6 7 8

British Library Cataloguing-in-Publication Data
A catalogue record for this book is available from the British Library.

ISBN 978-1407-18314-5

Printed and bound by Bell & Bain Ltd, Glasgow

Authors
Grammar, Punctuation and Spelling: Shelley Welsh
Reading: Giles Clare
Maths: Paul Hollin

Editorial
Rachel Morgan, Vicki Yates, Kate Pedlar, Kate Baxter, Suzanne Adams, Gemma Smith

Design
Nicolle Thomas, Neil Salt, Dan Prescott/Couper Street Type Co and Jayne Rawlings/
Oxford Raw Design

Cover Illustration
Adam Linley @ Beehive Illustration

Illustration
Karen Donnelly/D'Avila Illustration Agency

Technical artwork
Darren Lingard/D'Avila Illustration Agency

Acknowledgements
The publishers gratefully acknowledge permission to reproduce the following copyright material:

Laura Sheridan for the use of 'Dinomate' from *Dinosaur Poems* chosen by Paul Cookson. Text
© Laura Sheridan (Scholastic, 2015)

Photograph
page 24: Francesca Simon, Jeff Morgan/Alamy Stock Photo

Contents

How to use this book

This book contains three grammar, punctuation and spelling tests, three reading tests and two sets of maths tests for Year 3. Each test contains SATs-style questions. The tests provide a wide coverage of the test frameworks for this age group.

Grammar, punctuation and spelling

It is intended that children will take around ten minutes to complete each test. Each test is in two parts and comprises 11 or 12 grammar and punctuation questions and four spelling questions. For example, Grammar and Punctuation Test 1 and Spelling Test 1 make up one full test which should take ten minutes to complete.

Grammar and punctuation tests
Each test comprises 11 or 12 questions, which amount to 12 marks in total. Some questions require a selected response, where children select the correct answer from a list. Other questions require a constructed response, where children insert a word or punctuation mark, or write a short answer of their own.

Spelling tests
There are four questions in each test, which amount to four marks. Read each spelling number followed by *The word is...* Read the context sentence and then repeat *The word is...* Leave at least a 12-second gap between spellings. More information can be found on page 61.

Reading

Each test comprises a text followed by comprehension questions. There is one fiction, one non-fiction and one poetry text. It is intended that children will take approximately ten minutes to complete each test. Some questions require a selected response, where children choose the correct answer from several options. Other questions require a constructed response, where children write a short or extended answer of their own.

Maths

It is intended that children will take approximately ten minutes to complete each individual test; or approximately 30 minutes to complete each set of three tests. Some questions require a selected response, for example where children choose the correct answer from several options. Other questions require a constructed response, where children work out and write down their own answer.

Marking the tests

A mark scheme and a progress chart are also included towards the end of this book. After your child has completed a test, mark it and together identify and practise any areas where your child is less confident. Ask them to complete the next test at a later date, when you feel they have had enough time to practise and improve.

Marks

1. Underline the **three nouns** in the sentence below.

Bella was reading her book at the table.

1

2. What is the name of the **punctuation mark** that is missing from the sentence below?

How old is your dog

Tick **one**.

a question mark ☐

a full stop ☐

an exclamation mark ☐

an apostrophe ☐

1

3. Tick **two** boxes to show where the **commas** should go in the sentence below.

☐ ☐ ☐ ☐
↓ ↓ ↓ ↓

Alex handed out the maths books pencils rubbers and sharpeners.

1

10 MINS

Marks

4. What type of word is <u>thought</u> in the sentence below?

Zainab thought long and hard about the answer to the question.

Tick **one**.

a noun ☐

a verb ☐

an adverb ☐

an adjective ☐

1

5. Insert an appropriate **conjunction** in the sentence below.

Our teacher was cross _____ we were making too much noise.

1

6. Which sentence below is a **statement**?

Tick **one**.

Have you ever been to France? ☐

Paris is the capital of France. ☐

Look at this map of Paris. ☐

What a huge city it is! ☐

1

Marks

7. Write either <u>a</u> or <u>an</u> in the spaces to complete the sentence below.

Dad peeled _____ orange and _____ banana and added them to the fruit salad.

1

8. Which sentence below is written in the **past tense**?

Tick **one**.

I like vegetables but my sister doesn't. ☐

Max is going to the cinema with his cousin. ☐

Cornelia thinks she is getting a cold. ☐

Yesterday, I went to Ffion's for tea. ☐

1

9. Match each **prefix** to a word on the right to make a new word.

One has been done for you.

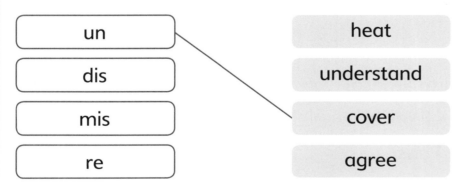

un	heat
dis	understand
mis	cover
re	agree

1

10 MINS

Marks

10. Add the **suffix** 's' or 'es' to make each word **plural**. Write the plural form on the line next to each word.

wish _____

boy _____

class _____

1

11. Which sentence below uses **capital letters** correctly?

Tick **one**.

Sara and karl are going to London next week. ☐

Sara and Karl are going to London next Week. ☐

Sara and Karl are going to London next week. ☐

Sara and Karl are going to london next week. ☐

1

12. Insert the missing **inverted commas** in the sentence below.

Please tidy your tables, then sit on the carpet, said Mrs Thomas.

1

Well done! END OF GRAMMAR & PUNCTUATION TEST 1!

Grammar and Punctuation
Test 2

10 MINS

Marks

1. Underline the **verb** in the sentence below.

Misha spent all her pocket money on my birthday present.

1

2. Tick the sentence that uses **tense** correctly.

Tick **one**.

Mum and I went shopping and we buy some new shoes. ☐

I have been to Wales but I hadn't been to Ireland. ☐

Raj came back from holiday tomorrow. ☐

As I hadn't eaten any breakfast, I was hungry at lunchtime. ☐

1

3. Insert a suitable **adverb** in the sentence below.

Gemma shouted _____ when the team scored a goal.

1

10. Add the **suffix** 's' or 'es' to make each word **plural**. Write the plural form on the line next to each word.

wish _____

boy _____

class _____

Marks

1

11. Which sentence below uses **capital letters** correctly?

Tick **one**.

Sara and karl are going to London next week. ☐

Sara and Karl are going to London next Week. ☐

Sara and Karl are going to London next week. ☐

Sara and Karl are going to london next week. ☐

1

12. Insert the missing **inverted commas** in the sentence below.

Please tidy your tables, then sit on the carpet, said Mrs Thomas.

1

Well done! END OF GRAMMAR & PUNCTUATION TEST 1!

Grammar and Punctuation
Test 2

10 MINS

Marks

1. Underline the **verb** in the sentence below.

Misha spent all her pocket money on my birthday present.

1

2. Tick the sentence that uses **tense** correctly.

Tick **one**.

Mum and I went shopping and we buy some new shoes. ☐

I have been to Wales but I hadn't been to Ireland. ☐

Raj came back from holiday tomorrow. ☐

As I hadn't eaten any breakfast, I was hungry at lunchtime. ☐

1

3. Insert a suitable **adverb** in the sentence below.

Gemma shouted _____ when the team scored a goal.

1

4. Tick the sentence below that is an **exclamation**.

Marks

Tick **one**.

How wonderful it is to see you ☐

How long is it since we last met ☐

Let me see if I have a photo of you ☐

You've certainly grown tall ☐

1

5. a. Insert the missing **apostrophe** to show a missing letter in the sentence below.

"I think its time I went to bed," said Norr.

1

b. Insert the missing **apostrophe** to show possession.

"You must be tired," said Norrs mum. "I normally have to chase you upstairs!"

1

6. Add a **prefix** to each word below to make its opposite meaning. Use each prefix only once.

_____regular

_____forgivable

| un | dis | ir |

_____obey

1

10 MINS

Marks

7. Underline the **noun phrase** in the sentence below.

We ordered a massive mushroom pizza.

1

8. Insert a suitable **preposition** to show where Dad left his car keys.

Dad left his car keys _____ the table.

1

9. Circle the **two** words that show a **continuous action** in the **present tense**.

Our teacher is marking our homework.

1

10. Draw a line to match each word on the left to a **suffix** that turns it into a **noun.**

garden		ion
enjoy		er
possess		ment

1

10 MINS

Marks

11. Tick **one** box in each row to show whether the underlined words are a **main clause** or a **subordinate clause**.

Sentence	Main clause	Subordinate clause
<u>We couldn't go to our swimming lesson</u> because Mum's car was broken.		
Gran took us to the park <u>even though it was starting to rain</u>.		
As we turned the corner, <u>we could see our new home for the next two weeks</u>.		

1

Well done! END OF GRAMMAR & PUNCTUATION TEST 2!

Grammar and Punctuation

Test 3

10 MINS

Marks

1. Circle the **adverb** in the sentence below.

Jan hastily tidied her room when she heard her mum coming.

1

2. Add a different **prefix** to each word below to make a different word. One has been done for you.

*auto***biography**

_____market

_____clockwise

_____marine

1

3. Tick **one** box to show where an **apostrophe** should go to indicate a missing letter or letters.

We cheered when our parents said theyd booked a caravan for three days.

1

Marks

4. What is the name of the underlined word in the sentence below?

Sadly, we can't go camping <u>as</u> a storm is forecast.

Tick **one**.

an adjective ☐

a preposition ☐

a prefix ☐

a conjunction ☐

1

5. Copy each word on the right into the table so that it is in the correct **word family**.

inform	informed	
really	realise	
medicine	medical	

paramedic

information

realistic

1

6. Draw a line to match each sentence on the left to its correct **function** on the right.

Wear your best shoes.	statement
Does the party start at 6 o'clock?	command
I'm wearing my new dress.	exclamation
How surprised he'll be to see us!	question

1

15

Marks

7. Tick **one** box in each row to show whether the sentence is written in the **present** or the **past tense**.

Sentence	Present tense	Past tense
I've written a letter to my Nan.		
We eat breakfast at 8 o'clock.		
There are 25 pupils in my class.		

1

8. Rewrite the sentence so that it uses correct grammar.

Matt done his homework on Saturday morning.

_____

_____

1

9. Look at where the arrow is pointing. Which **punctuation** mark is missing?

↓

"The bus is late today, said Faisal.

Tick **one**.

a question mark	☐	inverted comma	☐
a full stop	☐	an apostrophe	☐

1

Marks

10. Underline the **three adjectives** in the sentence below.

Melanie was sad to hear that the old lady was ill.

1

11. Which sentence below contains a **noun phrase**?

Tick **one**.

Milly was very tired. ☐

She went to bed very late. ☐

It was going to be a long, exhausting day. ☐

She couldn't stop yawning. ☐

1

12. Which sentence below is **punctuated** correctly?

Tick **one**.

We had a choice of, apple pie, ice cream, jelly or fruit salad for dessert. ☐

We had a choice of apple pie, ice cream, jelly or fruit salad for dessert. ☐

We had a choice of apple pie, ice cream, jelly, or fruit salad for dessert. ☐

1

Well done! END OF GRAMMAR & PUNCTUATION TEST 3!

17

Spelling Test 1

Marks

1. My brother is in _____ again.

2. Our dog likes to _____ his bones.

3. Dad put my uniform in the washing _____.

4. Mum likes _____ stories.

4

Well done! END OF SPELLING TEST 1!

Spelling Test 2

Marks

1. I threw the ball and Fergal _____ it.

2. Our neighbour has _____ cats.

3. Max stuck his _____ on the wall.

4. I find _____ hard.

4

Well done! END OF SPELLING TEST 2!

Spelling Test 3

Marks

1. The dragon roared _____ at its attackers.

2. We bought some plasters from the _____.

3. The nurse gave me an _____ in my arm.

4. Bryn received a _____ for winning the race.

4

Well done! END OF SPELLING TEST 3!

The Smart Alec Phone

Ellie didn't like school much. Well, not lessons anyway. She was beginning to think her head was full. Every day, her teacher tried to stuff more strange words into it – prefixes and prepositions, digits and denominators – but Ellie could never remember what they meant. She lived for playtimes, when she could gossip with friends and race around the playground, her hair streaming out behind her.

It was Ellie's birthday. She only wanted one thing: a new phone. She raced downstairs and there on the kitchen table was a small box in glittery wrapping paper.

"Happy birthday, love," said her mum. "I hope you like it. I know it's not the latest but –"

"Thanks, Mum," said Ellie and she rushed back up to her room with the box. She smiled and tore off the paper. She paused. It was a phone, but not one of the models she had been hoping for. She opened the box warily. It was the ugliest, uncoolest thing she had ever seen. It was chunky, made of cheap plastic and it had sharp, square edges. Ellie turned it on. The screen was murky and low resolution. Ellie rolled her eyes and sighed.

Suddenly a tinny voice announced, "You ungrateful brat, Ellie. Don't pull that face, young lady."

Ellie almost dropped the phone in surprise. "Who said that?" she whispered.

"Me, of course," replied the phone. "Who d'you think?"

"Who are you and what are you doing inside my phone?" Ellie blurted.

"My name's Smart Alec Phone One and I'm riding a bicycle," the voice replied.

"Riding a bike?" repeated Ellie in confusion.

"No, of course I'm not," said the phone. "I'm a phone. Ask me anything because I know everything. Seriously. Everything."

"Wow, you're cool," said Ellie, beaming. "Alright, what's aaa... determinominator?"

"Oh dear, oh dear, there's no such thing. You must mean either a determiner or a denominator. Try to speak properly," the voice replied.

"You sound like my teacher," said Ellie, scowling.

"How insulting!" said the voice. "I calculate I am 857.6% smarter than your teacher."

Suddenly, Ellie had the most wonderful idea. "Hey, Smart Alec, can you copy my voice?"

"Obviously, Ellie. How does this sound?"

For a second time, Ellie almost dropped the phone in surprise. "Wow, even I thought that was me," she replied. "Today is going to be a fun day at school!"

Marks

1. a. Write one thing Ellie **doesn't** like about school.

_____

1

b. Write one thing Ellie **does** like about school.

_____

_____

1

2. Is Ellie excited about opening her present?

Tick **one**.

Yes ☐   No ☐

Explain how you can tell from the text.

_____

_____

_____

2

10 MINS

Marks

3. *The screen was murky and low resolution.*

What does the word <u>murky</u> mean in this sentence?

Tick **one**.

dirty ☐

dim ☐

misty ☐

bright ☐

1

4. Why does Ellie roll her eyes and sigh?

_____

_____

_____

_____

1

5. What is the name of Ellie's new phone?

_____

1

KEEP IT GOING!

6. The phone tells Ellie that it is *riding a bicycle*. Why?

Tick **one**.

It is a clever phone. ☐

It is being sarcastic. ☐

It is a terrible liar. ☐

It is confused. ☐

Marks

◯ 1

7. Why does Ellie nearly drop the phone for a second time?

_____

_____

_____

◯ 1

8. What do you think Ellie is planning to do to have *a fun day at school*?

Tick **one**.

She will hide in the playground after break. ☐

She will use her phone to copy her friends' voices. ☐

She will show her phone off to her teachers. ☐

She will get her phone to answer questions in her voice. ☐

◯ 1

Well done! END OF READING TEST 1!

23

Interview with Francesca Simon

Francesca Simon is the author of books about Horrid Henry and his brother, Peter. Henry and Peter do not get on with each other.

How did you get the idea for Horrid Henry?

I got the idea for Horrid Henry when a friend asked me to write a story about a horrid child. Horrid Henry was born on the spot. I also wanted to write about sibling rivalry and families where one child was considered 'perfect' and the other 'horrid'.

Is Horrid Henry based on a real child?

No, but I think there's a bit of Henry and Peter inside everyone.

Where do you get your ideas from?

I get my ideas from things that happen to me, or to people I know, or from my imagination. I think of ordinary situations, like birthday parties or getting nits, then add a 'horrid' twist. So if my son has to have an injection, I think of how Henry would behave.

How long does it take to write a Horrid Henry book?

Around 4 months.

Who is your favourite character?

I like Moody Margaret, because I was bossy like her when I was her age. But of course I love Henry and Peter. And Beefy Bert makes me laugh.

What's your favourite Horrid Henry story?

I usually like the one I'm writing at the moment the best, but old favourites include *Horrid Henry's Injection* and *Horrid Henry's Gets Rich Quick*. I'm scared of injections and it makes me laugh when I read it.

How do you get your characters' names?

I think of funny adjectives, like 'sour' or 'rude' and match names to them. I love alliteration and use it as much as possible.

Why did you want to be an author?

I've always enjoyed writing and started writing fairy tales when I was 8 years old, so it is never too early to start. I used to be a journalist but I became an author after my son Joshua was born in 1989. I started to get a lot of ideas and began writing them down. It did take me over a year to have my first book accepted, however. I started writing because I kept getting ideas – I think it's because I love reading and I was reading a lot of children's books to him.

Marks

1. Henry is called a *horrid child*. Circle **one** word that means the same as <u>horrid</u> when used to describe Henry.

ugly	delightful

unpleasant	embarrassing

1

2. If Henry is <u>horrid</u>, what is Peter?

_____

1

Marks

3. Where does the author get her ideas?

Tick **three.**

from ordinary situations ☐

from her imagination ☐

from other people's books ☐

from things that happen to people she knows ☐

from watching TV ☐

1

4. Roughly how many months does it take the author to write a book?

_____

_____

1

5. Who does the author think she was like when she was young? Explain why.

_____

_____

_____

_____

2

6. Which Horrid Henry story makes the author laugh about something she is scared of?

_____

1

10 MINS

Marks

7. The author uses alliteration for her characters' names. Draw lines to match each adjective to the correct name.

Adjective	Name
Sour	Bert
Perfect	Henry
Horrid	Susan
Beefy	Peter

1

8. Do you think Francesca Simon likes writing Horrid Henry books? Explain using evidence from the text.

_____

_____

_____

_____

_____

_____

_____

_____

2

Well done! END OF READING TEST 2!

Dinomate

It's hard if a dinosaur is your friend,
Your problems never seem to end –

To cram him in the car is an awful squeeze,
He seems to be all tail and knees.
He steams up the windows and dents the door
And the air-freshener just can't cope anymore.

It's hard with a dinosaur at your school,
He won't obey a single rule –

He thunders and stomps down corridors,
He eats his dinner and then eats yours.
In lessons he won't pay attention
And Miss can't keep him in detention.

It's hard with a dinosaur on your team,
To watch him play games is a scream –

When he kicks a football his claws go through it,
Give him a bat and he's apt to chew it.
He's rubbish in goal and poor at tennis
And with a volleyball he's a menace.

It's hard with a dinosaur hanging around,
It's hard with a dinosaur in your town,
It's hard with a dinosaur for a mate...
But on the other hand – it's great!

By Laura Sheridan

10 MINS

I. What damage does the dinosaur do to the car?

_____

_____

Marks

1

2. *And the air-freshener just can't cope anymore.*

What does this tell you about the dinosaur?

_____

1

Marks

3. Draw a line to match the dinosaur's bad behaviour to the place at school:

noisy   in the classroom

greedy   in the corridor

doesn't listen   in the canteen

2

4. To watch him play games is a scream –

What does it mean when you say something <u>is a scream</u>?

Tick **one**.

It's frightening. ☐

It's loud. ☐

It's good fun. ☐

It's naughty. ☐

1

5. Give **one** reason why the dinosaur is no good at football?

_____

1

KEEP IT
GOING!

Marks

6. What might the dinosaur do to a cricket bat?

_____

_____

_____

1

7. Look at the verse that begins: *When he kicks a football his claws go through it,*

Find and **copy** a word that means the same as <u>nuisance</u>?

_____

_____

1

8. Thinking about the whole poem, what is surprising about the ending?

_____

_____

_____

_____

2

Well done! END OF READING TEST 3!

Marks

1. $4 + 4 + 4 + 4 =$

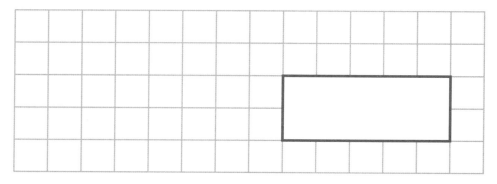

1

2. $20 - 13 =$

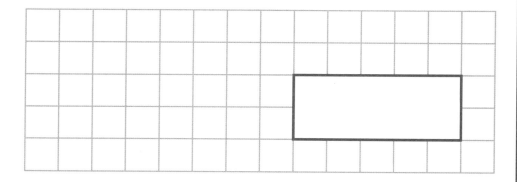

1

3. $\dfrac{1}{10} + \dfrac{1}{10} + \dfrac{1}{10} =$

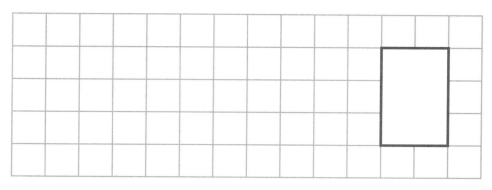

1

32

Marks

4. $8 \times 8 =$

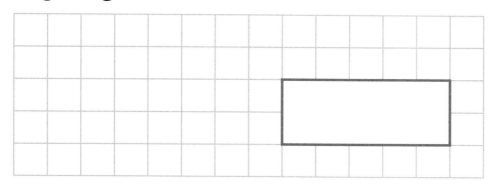

1

5. $376 - 50 =$

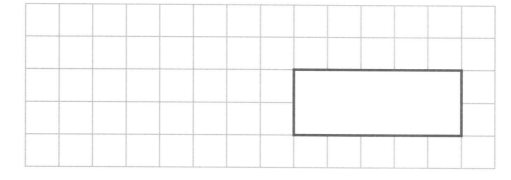

1

6. $1 - \frac{1}{4} =$

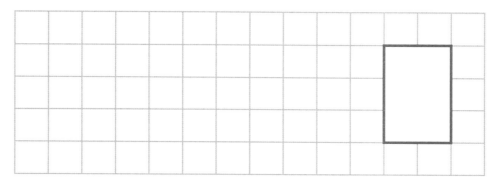

1

Marks

7. $24 \div \boxed{} = 3$

1

8. $60 \times 4 =$

1

10 MINS

Marks

9. 683 + 276 =

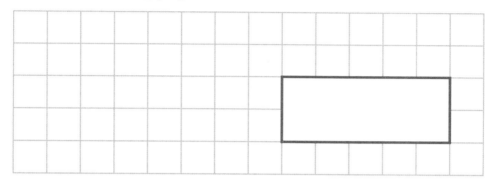

1

10.

Show your method

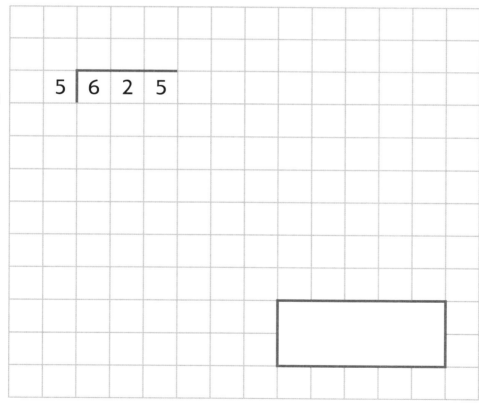

| 5 | 6 | 2 | 5 |

2

Well done! END OF MATHS SET A TEST 1!

Maths

Set A Test 2: Reasoning

Marks

I. Write the correct **digit** in each gap to complete these sentences.

The number 836 has _____ hundreds, _____ tens and _____ ones.

1

2. Write the missing digits to complete this addition.

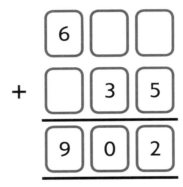

1

3. Judo club starts at 10.50am and finishes 55 minutes later. Draw the hands on the clocks to show the correct start and finish times.

Start

Finish

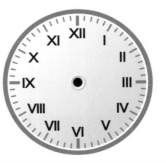

1

Marks

4. Which shape is an irregular shape? Explain why.

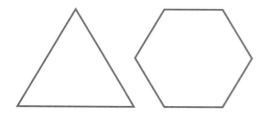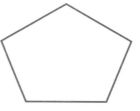

_____

_____

_____

_____

1

5. In an animal sanctuary, one-tenth of the animals are rabbits, two-tenths are guinea pigs and three-tenths are cats. All the other animals are dogs.

What **fraction** of the animals are dogs?

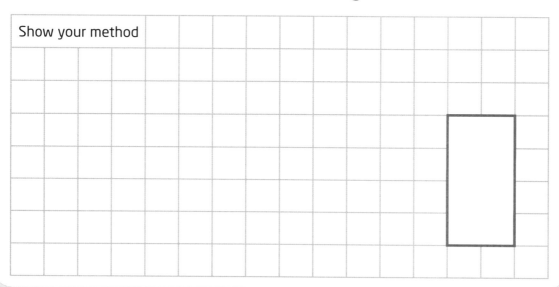

Show your method

2

6. Abdul buys some fruit.

Marks

one plum : 10p
one apple : 25p
one banana : 32p
two grapefruit : £1

Circle the coins Abdul must use to pay the correct amount.

1

7. A factory makes wooden stools.

To make one stool they need 1 seat, 3 legs and 8 nails.

Complete the chart below to help plan the work.

Number of stools	1	2	5	10	50	100
Seats	1	2				
Legs	3	6				
Nails	8	16				

1

Well done! END OF MATHS SET A TEST 2!

Maths
Set A Test 3: Reasoning

 **10 MINS**

Marks

I. A bag contains 8 counters of 3 different shapes.

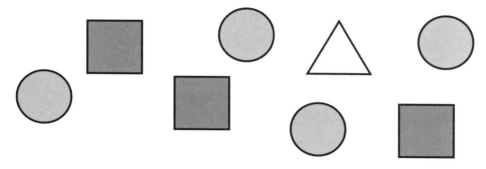

Write the correct **fractions**.

☐ of the counters are triangles, ☐ are circles,

and ☐ are squares.

1

---

2. Write the correct sign in each space: **<**, **>** or **=**.

67 ☐ sixty-seven

two hundred and eighty-three ☐ 243

seven hundred ☐ 790

1

39

Marks

3. There are 24 children in a class.

Their teacher wants to arrange them in different-sized groups for different lessons. Complete the chart to show the group sizes for each subject.

Subject	English	Maths	Art	PE	Music
Number of groups	3	4	6	8	12
Number of children in each group					

1

4. a. Anya draws around a wooden rectangle.

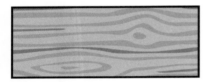

Using a ruler, find the perimeter of the shape Anya has drawn.

Perimeter = cm

1

b. Anya draws around the same shape four times in a pattern like this.

Calculate the perimeter of the new shape.

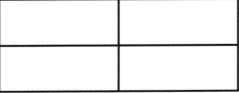

Not to scale.

Perimeter = cm

1

5. At the start of a fireworks display there are 576 people watching.

During the display 245 more people arrive and 384 people leave.

How many people are watching at the end?

Marks

Show your method

people

2

6. In a school survey, children asked their parents about their favourite online food delivery website.

The number of parents who liked Fresh Foods was halfway between those who liked Food 2 Home and those who liked Home Deli.

Complete the bar chart for all the parents who prefer the Fresh Foods website.

Marks

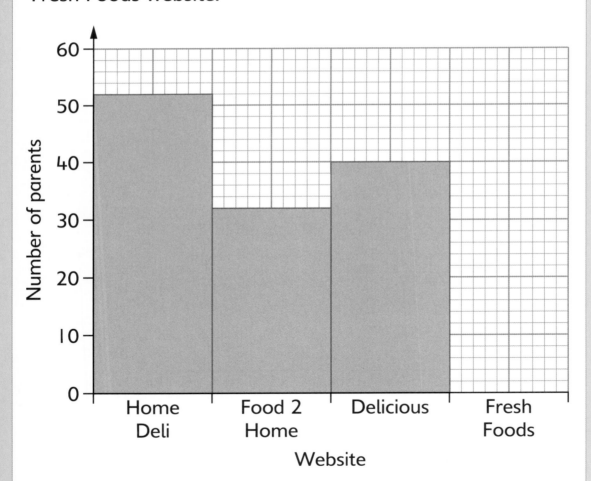

1

Well done! END OF MATHS SET A TEST 3!

Marks

1. $15 - 10 =$

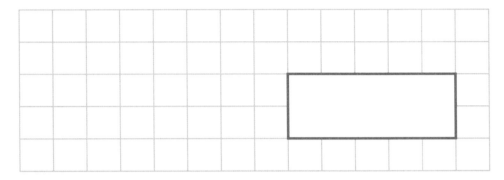

1

2. $\frac{1}{10} + \frac{1}{10} + \frac{1}{10} + \frac{1}{10} + \frac{1}{10} =$

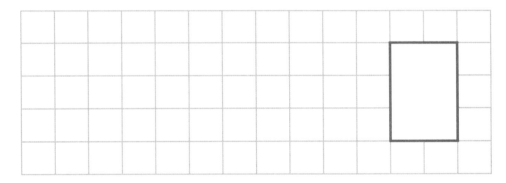

1

3. $24 \div 4 =$

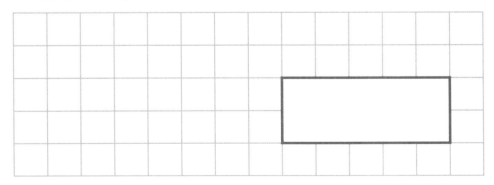

1

10 MINS

Marks

4. $600 ÷ 6 =$

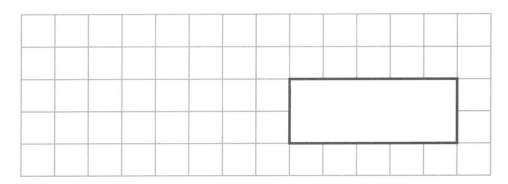

1

5. $295 + 8 =$

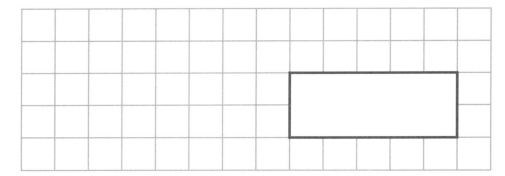

1

6. $50 + 50 + 50 + 50 + 50 =$

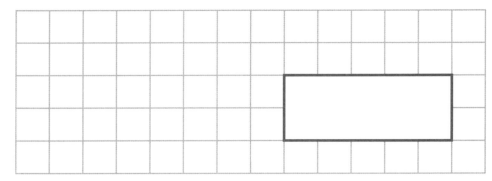

1

Marks

7. $12 \times \boxed{} = 36$

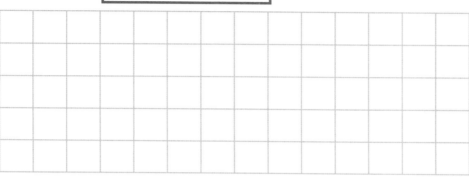

1

8. $110 \times 5 =$

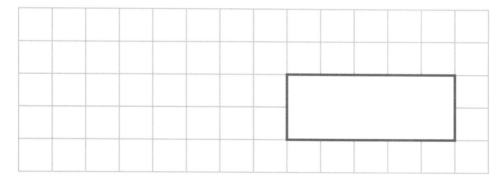

1

45

10 MINS

Marks

9. $836 - 409 =$

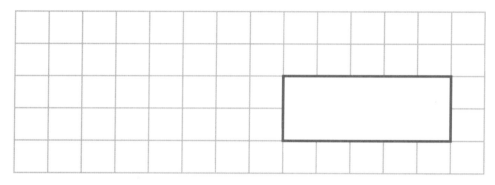

1

10. $54 \times 4 =$

Show your method

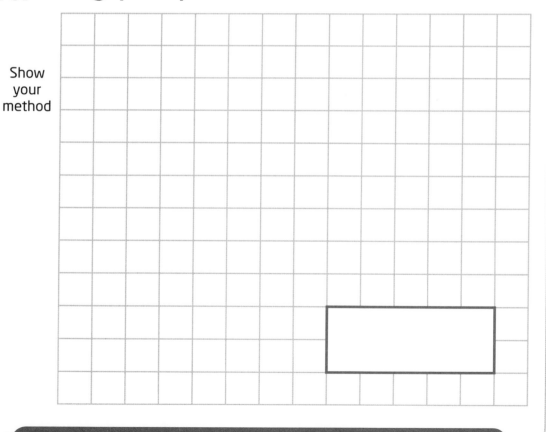

2

Well done! END OF MATHS SET B TEST 1!

Marks

1. Liu describes a parallelogram.

Tick the **three** statements he should use:

☐ The opposite sides are parallel.

☐ It has two pairs of equal sides.

☐ It has two right-angles.

☐ The opposite angles are equal.

☐ It has four equal sides.

1

2. Write 200, 500 and 750 on the number line.

```
   ├──────────────────┬──────────────────────────────┤
   0                                              1000
```

1

3. These two straight lines are perpendicular.

Using a ruler, draw one more straight line that will create two more right-angles, two more **perpendicular lines**, and one pair of **parallel lines**.

1

4. A fraction of the buttons in Set A has been circled.

Circle the equivalent fraction in Set B.

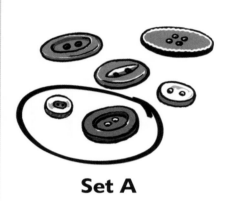

Set A

Set B

Marks

1

5. Write the mass of each of the pairs of fruit.

g

g

g

1

48

Marks

6. A school has three fetes per year to raise money.

This year's target is a total of £1000.

The Christmas fete raises £376 and the Easter fete raises £287.

How much will they have to raise at the summer fete to reach their target?

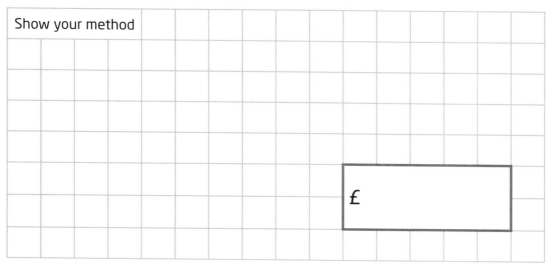

Show your method

£

2

7. A minibus has 18 seats.

Half of all the seats have girls sitting in them and one-third of all the seats have boys sitting in them.

One seat has a teacher sitting in it.

How many empty seats are there?

empty seats

1

Well done! END OF MATHS SET B TEST 2!

49

Maths

Set B Test 3: Reasoning

Marks

1. Harry places some fraction cards in a line.

Write a **>** or **<** sign in each box to make true statements.

One has been done for you.

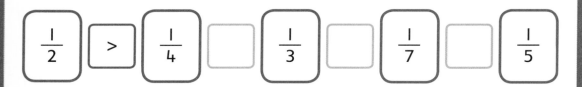

$\frac{1}{2}$ > $\frac{1}{4}$ ☐ $\frac{1}{3}$ ☐ $\frac{1}{7}$ ☐ $\frac{1}{5}$

1

---

2. Sophie starts at 50 and counts in multiples of 110.

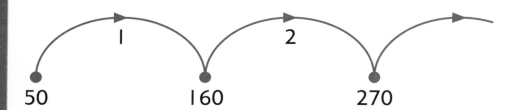

1   2

50   160   270

Which number will she reach on
her **fourth** count?

1

Marks

3. Write the missing digits to make this correct.

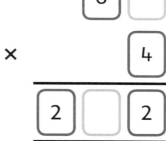

$$
\begin{array}{r}
6\ \square \\
\times \qquad 4 \\
\hline
2\ \square\ 2 \\
\hline
\end{array}
$$

1

4. The table shows the number of children in each school year who own certain pets.

	Year 3	Year 4	Year 5	Year 6
Cats	30	28	39	22
Dog	27	36	19	25
Guinea pig	6	4	13	10

a. Which year group owns the most pets? Year _____

b. Which is the most popular pet? _____

1

5. A round theatre has four identical seating areas and a balcony all the way round. The balcony has 100 seats.

The theatre holds 920 people altogether.

How many seats are there in any one of the other areas?

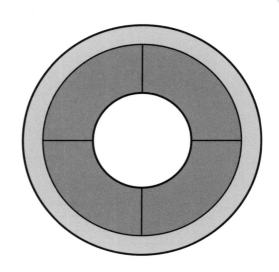

Marks

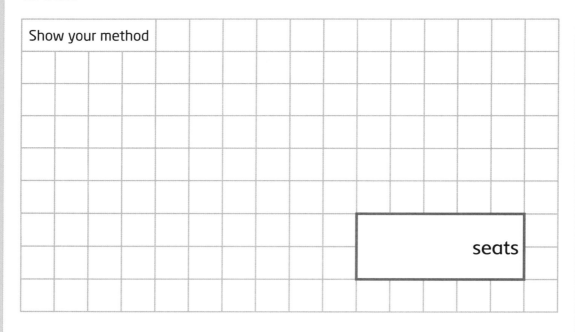

Show your method

seats

2

10 MINS

Marks

6. a. Four sisters' heights are measured.

Cath is 138cm, Helen is 168cm, Jess is 115cm, and Nina is 150cm.

Write the correct name under each sister.

_____ _____ _____ _____

1

b. How much taller is the tallest sister than the shortest sister?

cm

1

Well done! END OF MATHS SET B TEST 3!

Answers

Q	Mark scheme for Grammar and Punctuation Test 1	Marks
1	**Award 1 mark** if 'Bella', 'book' and 'table' are underlined. **Grammar essentials:** A noun is a naming word for a person, place, thing, animal, idea or concept.	1
2	**Award 1 mark** if 'a question mark' is ticked. **Punctuation essentials:** A question is a sentence that asks something. It ends with a question mark.	1
3	**Award 1 mark** if the second and third boxes are ticked. **Punctuation essentials:** Commas can be used to separate items in a list (but not before 'and').	1
4	**Award 1 mark** if 'a verb' is ticked. **Grammar essentials:** A verb is a word that names an action or a state of being.	1
5	**Award 1 mark** if an appropriate subordinating conjunction has been inserted, such as 'because' or 'as'. **Grammar essentials:** A subordinating conjunction introduces a subordinate clause. A subordinate clause is dependent on a main clause – it doesn't make sense on its own.	1
6	**Award 1 mark** if 'Paris is the capital of France.' is ticked. **Grammar essentials:** A statement is a sentence that tells you something.	1
7	**Award 1 mark** for: 'Dad peeled **an** orange and **a** banana and added them to the fruit salad.' **Grammar essentials:** A determiner indicates whether a noun is specific/known (e.g. 'the') or more general/unknown (e.g. 'a' or 'an'). The determiner 'an' comes before a noun that starts with a vowel.	1
8	**Award 1 mark** if 'Yesterday, I went to Ffion's for tea.' is ticked. **Grammar essentials:** The past tense describes an action that has happened.	1
9	**Award 1 mark** for: 'disagree', 'misunderstand', 'reheat'. **Grammar essentials:** A prefix is a string of letters added to the beginning of a word to turn it into another word. It does not alter the spelling of the word it is joined to.	1
10	**Award 1 mark** for: 'wishes', 'boys' and 'classes'. **Grammar essentials:** To make most nouns plural, simply add the suffix 's' or 'es'. Some nouns have an irregular plural form, such as 'children', 'men', 'mice'.	1
11	**Award 1 mark** if 'Sara and Karl are going to London next week.' is ticked. **Punctuation essentials:** Capital letters are used at the start of a sentence and at the start of proper nouns. Proper nouns include the names of people and places.	1
12	**Award 1 mark** for: "Please tidy your tables, then sit on the carpet," said Mrs Thomas. **Punctuation essentials:** In direct speech, inverted commas come at the start of the opening speech and after the final punctuation of the speech.	1
	Total	12

Q	Mark scheme for Grammar and Punctuation Test 2	Marks
1	**Award 1 mark** if 'spent' has been underlined. **Grammar essentials:** A verb is a word that names an action or a state of being.	1
2	**Award 1 mark** if 'As I hadn't eaten any breakfast, I was hungry at lunchtime.' is ticked. **Grammar essentials:** A verb's tense can be either present or past. There is no future tense. The future is made from the present tense.	1
3	**Award 1 mark** for insertion of a suitable adverb such as 'loudly' or 'wildly'. **Grammar essentials:** An adverb can give more information about the verb in a sentence.	1

54

Q	Mark scheme for Grammar and Punctuation Test 2 continued	Marks
4	**Award 1 mark** if 'How wonderful it is to see you' is ticked. **Grammar and punctuation essentials:** An exclamation sentence starts with 'How' or 'What', contains a verb and ends with an exclamation mark.	1
5	**Award 1 mark** for '"I think it's time I went to bed," said Norr. **Award 1 mark** for "You must be tired," said Norr's mum. "I normally have to chase you upstairs!" **Punctuation essentials:** An apostrophe can be used to indicate a missing letter or letters (contraction) or ownership (possession).	2
6	**Award 1 mark** for: 'irregular', 'unforgivable' and 'disobey'. **Grammar essentials:** A prefix is a string of letters added to the beginning of a word to turn it into another word. It does not alter the spelling of the word it is joined to.	1
7	**Award 1 mark** if 'a massive mushroom pizza' is underlined. **Grammar essentials:** A noun phrase is a group of words that add more information about a noun. The noun is the most important word in the phrase.	1
8	**Award 1 mark** if a suitable preposition has been inserted such as 'on', 'under' or 'beside'. **Grammar essentials:** A preposition links a noun, pronoun or noun phrase to another word in the sentence.	1
9	**Award 1 mark** if 'is marking' is circled. **Grammar essentials:** This verb tense is the present progressive and shows a continuous action in the present.	1
10	**Award 1 mark** for: 'gardener', 'enjoyment', 'possession'. **Grammar essentials:** A suffix is a letter or string of letters added to the end of a word to turn it into another word.	1
11	**Award 1 mark** if the rows are ticked in the following order: main clause, subordinate clause, main clause. **Grammar essentials:** A subordinate clause is introduced by a subordinating conjunction. It is dependent on a main clause – it doesn't make sense on its own.	1
	Total	12

Q	Mark scheme for Grammar and Punctuation Test 3	Marks
1	**Award 1 mark** if 'hastily' is circled. **Grammar essentials:** An adverb can give more information about the verb in a sentence.	1
2	**Award 1 mark** for: 'supermarket', 'anticlockwise' and 'submarine' or suitable alternatives. **Grammar essentials:** A prefix is a string of letters added to the beginning of a word to turn it into another word. It does not alter the spelling of the word it is joined to.	1
3	**Award 1 mark** for a tick in the box with the arrow pointing to 'they'd'. **Punctuation essentials:** An apostrophe can indicate a missing letter or letters (contraction).	1
4	**Award 1 mark** if 'a conjunction' is ticked. **Grammar essentials:** Here, the word 'as' is a subordinating conjunction, introducing a subordinate clause.	1
5	**Award 1 mark** for a correctly completed table: | inform	informed	**information**
really	realise	**realistic**
medicine	medical	**paramedic** | **Grammar essentials:** A word family is a group of words that share the same root.	1

Q	Mark scheme for Grammar and Punctuation Test 3 continued	Marks
6	**Award 1 mark** for: 'Wear your best shoes.' – command; 'Does the party start at 6 o'clock?' – question; 'I'm wearing my new dress.' – statement; 'How surprised he'll be to see us!' – exclamation. **Grammar essentials:** A command is a sentence that tells you to do something and usually ends with a full stop. A question asks you to do something and ends with a question mark. A statement tells you something and ends with a full stop. An exclamation starts with 'How' or 'What', contains a verb and ends with an exclamation mark.	1
7	**Award 1 mark** for each row ticked in the following order: past tense, present tense, present tense. **Grammar essentials:** The past tense tells you about something that has happened. The present tense tells you about something that is happening now or happens on a regular basis.	1
8	**Award 1 mark** for: 'Matt did his homework on Saturday morning.' **Grammar essentials:** The word 'done' is incorrect grammar. In Standard English, we use correct grammar.	1
9	**Award 1 mark** if 'inverted comma' is ticked. **Punctuation essentials:** In direct speech, inverted commas come at the start of the speech and after the final punctuation of the speech.	1
10	**Award 1 mark** if 'sad', 'old' and 'ill' are underlined. **Grammar essentials:** An adjective can come before the noun, to modify it, or after the verb 'to be' as its complement.	1
11	**Award 1 mark** if 'It was going to be a long, exhausting day.' is ticked. **Grammar essentials:** A noun phrase is a group of words that adds more information about a noun. The noun is the most important word in the phrase.	1
12	**Award 1 mark** if 'We had a choice of apple pie, ice cream, jelly or fruit salad for dessert.' is ticked. **Punctuation essentials:** Commas can be used to separate items in a list (but not before 'or' in a list).	1
	Total	12

Q	Mark scheme for Reading Test 1: The Smart Alec Phone	Marks
1	**a. Award 1 mark** for: lessons **b. Award 1 mark** for one of: playtimes; gossiping with friends; racing around the playground	1 1
2	**Award 2 marks** for 'Yes' ticked and two examples of Ellie's excited behaviour. For example: She rushes back upstairs and tears off the paper. **Award 1 mark** for 'Yes' ticked and one example. For example: She races downstairs to the kitchen. Do not accept 'No' ticked, with or without an explanation.	2
3	**Award 1 mark** for: dim	1
4	**Award 1 mark** for answers referring to Ellie's disappointment. For example: She is annoyed that she didn't get the right phone.	1
5	**Award 1 mark** for: Smart Alec Phone One	1
6	**Award 1 mark** for: It is being sarcastic.	1
7	**Award 1 mark** for answers such as: She is surprised because Smart Alec sounds just like her.	1
8	**Award 1 mark** for: She will get her phone to answer questions in her voice.	1
	Total	10

Q	Mark scheme for Reading Test 2: Interview with Francesca Simon	Marks
1	**Award 1 mark** for: unpleasant	1
2	**Award 1 mark** for: perfect	1
3	**Award 1 mark** for all three correctly ticked: from ordinary situations; from her imagination; from things that happen to people she knows.	1
4	**Award 1 mark** for: 4 or four	1
5	**Award 2 marks** for: Moody Margaret, because she was bossy when she was young. **Award 1 mark** for Moody Margaret without explanation.	2

Q	Mark scheme for Reading Test 2: Interview with Francesca Simon continued	Marks
6	**Award 1 mark** for: *Horrid Henry's Injection*	1
7	**Award 1 mark** for all correct: Sour ⟶ Susan Perfect ⟶ Peter Horrid ⟶ Henry Beefy ⟶ Bert	1
8	**Award 2 marks** for answers referring to the author's enjoyment and two pieces of relevant evidence from the text. For example: She does enjoy it because she says she has always enjoyed writing. She also says she likes the story when she is writing it. **Award 1 mark** for answers referring to the author's enjoyment and one piece of relevant evidence from the text. For example: I think she does because she used to be a journalist and now she's a writer.	2
	Total	10

Q	Mark scheme for Reading Test 3: Dinomate	Marks
1	**Award 1 mark** for: He dents the door.	1
2	**Award 1 mark** for answers referring to how much the dinosaur must smell. For example: He must be really smelly.	1
3	**Award 2 marks** for all 3 answers correctly matched: noisy ⟶ in the corridor greedy ⟶ in the canteen doesn't listen ⟶ in the classroom **Award 1 mark** for one answer correctly matched.	2
4	**Award 1 mark** for: It's good fun.	1
5	**Award 1 mark** for: His claws go through the football. Do not accept: He's rubbish in goal. (There's no reason given.)	1
6	**Award 1 mark** for: He might chew it.	1
7	**Award 1 mark** for: menace	1
8	**Award 2 marks** for answers referring to how it is still good to have a dinosaur for a friend despite all the problems. For example: The writer still thinks it's great to have a dinosaur friend but the rest of the poem is about all the problems it causes. **Award 1 mark** for answers referring to it being good to have a dinosaur friend, without comparing this to the rest of the poem.	2
	Total	10

Q	Mark scheme for Maths Set A Test 1: Arithmetic	Marks
1	16	1
2	7	1
3	$\frac{3}{10}$	1
4	64	1
5	326	1
6	$\frac{3}{4}$	1
7	8	1
8	240	1
9	959	1
10	125 **Award 1 mark** for a correct method but one arithmetical error.	2
	Total	11

Q	Mark scheme for Maths Set A Test 2: Reasoning	Marks
1	The number 836 has **8** hundreds, **3** tens and **6** ones.	1
2	$$\begin{array}{r} 6\ \ \mathbf{6}\ \ 7 \\ +\ \ \mathbf{2}\ \ 3\ \ 5 \\ \hline 9\ \ 0\ \ 2 \end{array}$$	1
3	The clocks should show 10.50 and 11.45. Minute and hour hands should be easily distinguishable. The minute hands should be accurate to one minute, and the hour hands within the correct 'half' of the sector they would move within on an analogue clock.	1
4	The pentagon is the irregular shape. It is irregular because some sides and angles are different to others. All of the other shapes have sides that are the same length and angles that are the same size – they are all regular. Accept any explanation that identifies the pentagon and explains how it is different from the other shapes.	1
5	$\frac{4}{10}$ of the animals are dogs. Accept $\frac{2}{5}$. **Award 1 mark** for a clear demonstration of correct procedure for adding and subtracting fractions but with a maximum of one arithmetical error.	2
6	**Award 1 mark for** any combination of coins that totals £1 and 67p.	1

Number of stools	1	2	5	10	50	100
Seats	1	2	**5**	**10**	**50**	**100**
Legs	3	6	**15**	**30**	**150**	**300**
Nails	8	16	**40**	**80**	**400**	**800**

Q 7 — Marks 1

		Total	**8**

Q	Mark scheme for Maths Set A Test 3: Reasoning	Marks
1	$\frac{1}{8}$ of the counters are triangles, $\frac{4}{8}$ are circles, and $\frac{3}{8}$ are squares. Accept $\frac{1}{2}$ for circles.	1
2	67 **=** sixty-seven two hundred and eighty-three **>** 243 seven hundred **<** 790	1

Subject	English	Maths	Art	PE	Music
Number of groups	3	4	6	8	12
Number of children in each group	8	6	4	3	2

Q 3 — Marks 1

4	**a.** Perimeter = 14cm **b.** Perimeter = 28cm	1 1

Q	Mark scheme for Maths Set A Test 3: Reasoning continued	Marks
5	437 people **Award 1 mark** for a correct method but with a maximum of one arithmetical error.	2
6	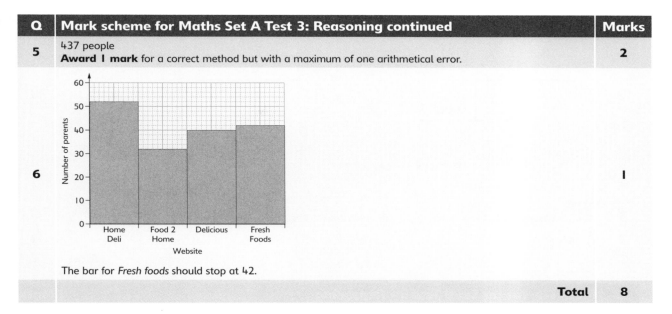 The bar for *Fresh foods* should stop at 42.	1
	Total	**8**

Q	Mark scheme for Maths Set B Test 1: Arithmetic	Marks
1	5	1
2	$\frac{5}{10}$ or $\frac{1}{2}$	1
3	6	1
4	100	1
5	303	1
6	250	1
7	3	1
8	550	1
9	427	1
10	216 **Award 1 mark** for a correct method but one arithmetical error.	2
	Total	**11**

Q	Mark scheme for Maths Set B Test 2 – Reasoning	Marks
1	**Award 1 mark** for all three correctly ticked: The opposite sides are parallel. It has two pairs of equal sides. The opposite angles are equal.	1
2	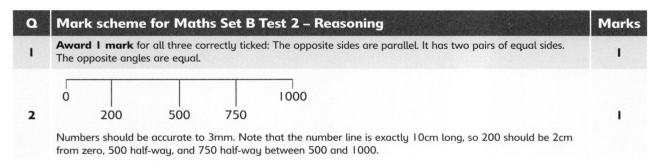 Numbers should be accurate to 3mm. Note that the number line is exactly 10cm long, so 200 should be 2cm from zero, 500 half-way, and 750 half-way between 500 and 1000.	1

3	or	1
4	Any five buttons clearly circled. Award mark only if amount is unambiguous.	1
5	150g 350g 400g	1
6	£337 **Award 1 mark** for a correct method but with a maximum of one arithmetical error.	2
7	2 empty seats	1
	Total	8

Q	Mark scheme for Set B Test 3 – Reasoning	Marks
1	$\frac{1}{2} > \frac{1}{4} < \frac{1}{3} > \frac{1}{7} < \frac{1}{5}$	1
2	490	1
3	$\begin{array}{r} 6\ 3 \\ \times \quad\quad 4 \\ \hline 2\ 5\ 2 \\ \hline \end{array}$	1
4	**a.** Year 5 **b.** Cats	1
5	205 seats **Award 1 mark** for a correct approach with a maximum of one arithmetical error.	2
6	**a.** Helen Jess Nina Cath **b.** 53cm	1 1
	Total	8

How to administer the spelling tests

There are three short spelling tests in this book with four questions in each test. Grammar and Punctuation Test 1 and Spelling Test 1 make up one full test which should take ten minutes in total to complete. However, you should allow your child as much time as they need.

Read the instructions in the box below. The instructions are similar to the ones given in the National Curriculum tests. This will familiarise children with the style and format of the tests and show them what to expect.

Listen carefully to the instructions I am going to give you.

I am going to read four sentences to you. Each sentence on your answer sheet has a missing word. Listen carefully to the missing word and write it in the space provided, making sure you spell the word correctly.

I will read the word, then the word within the sentence, then repeat the word a third time.

Do you have any questions?

Read the spellings as follows:

- Give the question number, 'Spelling 1'
- Say, 'The word is...'
- Read the whole sentence to show the word in context
- Repeat, 'The word is...'

Leave at least a 12-second gap between each spelling.

At the end re-read all four questions. Then say, 'This is the end of the test. Please put down your pencil or pen.'

Each correct answer should be awarded **1 mark**.

Spelling test transcripts

Spelling Test 1

Spelling 1: The word is **trouble**.
My brother is in **trouble** again.
The word is **trouble**.

Spelling 2: The word is **bury**.
Our dog likes to **bury** his bones.
The word is **bury**.

Spelling 3: The word is **machine**.
Dad put my uniform in the washing **machine**.
The word is **machine**.

Spelling 4: The word is **mystery**.
Mum likes **mystery** stories.
The word is **mystery**.

Spelling Test 2

Spelling 1: The word is **caught**.
I threw the ball and Fergal **caught** it.
The word is **caught**.

Spelling 2: The word is **eight**.
Our neighbour has **eight** cats.
The word is **eight**.

Spelling 3: The word is **picture**.
Max stuck his **picture** on the wall.
The word is **picture**.

Spelling 4: The word is **division**.
I find **division** hard.
The word is **division**.

Spelling Test 3

Spelling 1: The word is **angrily**.
The dragon roared **angrily** at its attackers.
The word is **angrily**.

Spelling 2: The word is **chemist**.
We bought some plasters from the **chemist**.
The word is **chemist**.

Spelling 3: The word is **injection**.
The nurse gave me an **injection** in my arm.
The word is **injection**.

Spelling 4: The word is **medal**.
Bryn received a **medal** for winning the race.
The word is **medal**.

Progress chart

Fill in your score in the table below to see how well you've done.

	Score	Percentage
Grammar, Punctuation and Spelling Test 1	/12	
Grammar, Punctuation and Spelling Test 2	/12	
Grammar, Punctuation and Spelling Test 3	/12	
Reading Test 1	/10	
Reading Test 2	/10	
Reading Test 3	/10	
Maths Set A: Test 1		
Maths Set A: Test 2	/27	
Maths Set A: Test 3		
Maths Set B: Test 1		
Maths Set B: Test 2	/27	
Maths Set B: Test 3		

Percentage	
0–33%	Good try! You need more practice in some topics – ask an adult to help you.
34–69%	You're doing really well. Ask for extra help for any topics you found tricky.
70–100%	You're a 10-Minute SATs Test star – good work!

Reward Certificate

Well done!

You have completed all of the 10-Minute SATs Tests

Name: _____   Date: _____

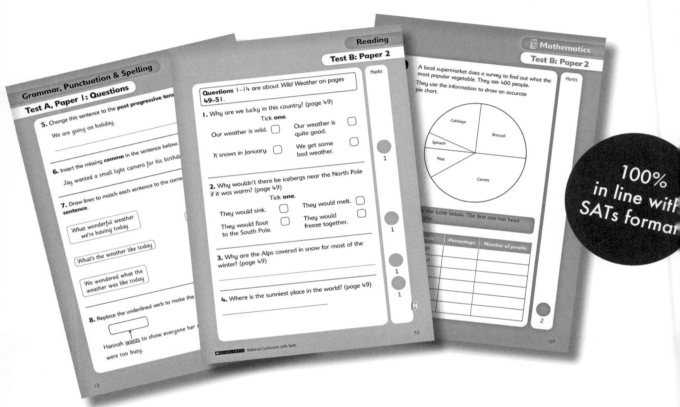